GET INVOLVED

ENVIRONMENTAL ACTIVIST

Carrie Gleason

Be a Junior Activist

🌱
Crabtree Publishing Company
www.crabtreebooks.com

Crabtree Publishing Company
www.crabtreebooks.com

For today's activists, who need to know and remember the past in order to make a better tomorrow.

Developed and produced by Plan B Book Packagers

Author:
Carrie Gleason

Art Director:
Rosie Gowsell-Pattison

Editorial Director:
Ellen Rodger

Production Coordinator:
Margaret Amy Salter

Editor:
Molly Aloian

Proofreader:
Kathy Middleton

Photographs:
© Carson Baldwin Jr./Animals Animals - Earth Scenes: front cover
Darryl Dyck/The Canadian Press: p. 26
Bettmann/Corbis: p. 21
Gustavo Gilabert/Corbis Saba: p. 7
Shutterstock: luminouslens: cover (paper); Peter Baxter: p. 1; roadk: p. 3; Jeff R. Clow: p. 4 (top); miljko: p. 4 (bottom); Andrejs Pidjass: p. 5; goldenangel: p. 6 (bottom); Happy Alex: p. 6 (top); Michael Zysman: p. 8; Colour: p. 9 (top); Pakhnyushcha: p. 9 (bottom); Copit: p. 10; Albert H. Teich: p. 11; Ken Brown: p. 12 (top); MdN: p. 12 (bottom); Pedro Miguel Nunes: p. 13 (bottom); Mikhail Olykainen: p. 13 (top); Pablo H Caridad: p. 14; Nik Niklz: p. 15 (bottom); stavklem: p. 15 (top); Jeff Banke: p. 16; Natali_ua: p. 17 (top); Creasence: p. 18 (bottom); Emin Kuliyev: p. 18 (top); Lowe Llaguno: p. 19 (bottom); Sylvana Rega: p. 19 (top); Elnur: p. 20 (top); foment: p. 20 (bottom); rfx: p. 22; sculpies: p. 23; Mark R: p. 24; Kushch Dmitry: p. 25 (left); Muriel Lasure: p. 25 (right); stocklight: p. 27; Shutterlist: p. 28 (top); sn4ke: p. 28 (bottom); Jeff Davies: p. 29; Crystal Kirk: p. 31

Field Notes credits:
p. 5: from the South African Bill of Rights; p. 7: Julia Butterfly Hill quotation courtesy of E/The Environmental Magazine; p. 11: Bob Hunter quotation courtesy of Greenpeace (www.greenpeace.org); p. 19: Gaylord Nelson quotation courtesy of the Milwaukee Journal Sentinal; p. 25: Dr. Robert Bullard quotation courtesy of Earth First! Journal.

Cover: Young activists work to save a loon after an oil spill.

Title page: An environmentalist examines the quality of water in a pond.

Publisher's note to teachers and parents
Although careful consideration has been made in selecting the list of Web sites, due to the nature of the subjects' content some Web sites may contain or have a link to content and images of a sensitive nature. The views and opinions presented in these Web sites are those of the organization and do not represent the views and policies of Crabtree Publishing. As Web site content and addresses often change, Crabtree Publishing accepts no liability for the content of the Web sites.

Library and Archives Canada Cataloguing in Publication

Gleason, Carrie, 1973-
 Environmental activist / Carrie Gleason.

(Get involved!)
Includes index.
ISBN 978-0-7787-4694-2 (bound).--ISBN 978-0-7787-4706-2 (pbk.)

 1. Environmentalists--Juvenile literature. 2. Environmentalism--Juvenile literature. 3. Environmental protection--Juvenile literature. I. Title.
II. Series: Get involved!

GE195.5.G54 2010   j333.72   C2009-901928-0

Library of Congress Cataloging-in-Publication Data

Gleason, Carrie.
 Environmental activist / Carrie Gleason.
   p. cm. -- (Get involved!)
Includes index.
ISBN 978-0-7787-4706-2 (pbk. : alk. paper) -- ISBN 978-0-7787-4694-2 (reinforced library binding : alk. paper)
 1. Environmentalists--Juvenile literature. 2. Environmentalism--Juvenile literature. I. Title. II. Series.

GE80.G54 2010
333.72--dc22
                                                            2009013090

Crabtree Publishing Company

www.crabtreebooks.com   1-800-387-7650

Copyright © 2010 CRABTREE PUBLISHING COMPANY. All rights reserved. No part of this publication may be reproduced, stored in a retrieval system or be transmitted in any form or by any means, electronic, mechanical, photocopying, recording, or otherwise, without the prior written permission of Crabtree Publishing Company. In Canada: We acknowledge the financial support of the Government of Canada through the Book Publishing Industry Development Program (BPIDP) for our publishing activities.

Published in Canada
Crabtree Publishing
616 Welland Ave.
St. Catharines, ON
L2M 5V6

Published in the United States
Crabtree Publishing
PMB16A
350 Fifth Ave., Suite 3308
New York, NY 10118

Published in the United Kingdom
Crabtree Publishing
White Cross Mills
High Town, Lancaster
LA1 4XS

Published in Australia
Crabtree Publishing
386 Mt. Alexander Rd.
Ascot Vale (Melbourne)
VIC 3032

Contents

Environmental rights	4
What is an activist?	6
How much is too much?	8
Living green	10
A short history	12
On the land	16
The air we breathe	18
Dirty water	20
Energy in need	22
Environmental justice	24
In the trenches	26
What you can do	28
Saving the planet	30
Glossary and Index	32

GET INVOLVED!

Environmental rights

Environmentalism is a concern for the well-being of the environment. It is about protecting the environment from pollution and destruction. Environmentalists are activists who encourage others to change their attitudes and form habits that benefit the environment. They also pressure governments to create better environmental laws.

Environmental rights

Everyone should have the right to live in a safe environment. Environmental rights include the right to clean air and water and the right to live in an environment that is not harmful to health.

Are you concerned about the quality of the air you breathe and the water you drink? Are you surprised by the amount of garbage we produce and that companies continue to sell products with too much packaging? Are you worried about global warming? If so, environmentalism might be a cause for you.

Environmental activists are concerned for the well-being of the environment.

Human activity, such as burning tires at a dump site, contributes to pollution that harms our air quality.

Field Notes:

The country of South Africa has made environmental rights part of its Bill of Rights. A Bill of Rights is a list of basic freedoms a country guarantees its citizens. According to South Africa's Bill of Rights, environmental rights are a part of **human rights** and are something all South Africans are **entitled** to. Here's what their Bill of Rights says, with some explanation of the difficult terms:

Everyone has the right:

1. to an environment that is not harmful to their health or well-being; and
2. to have the environment protected, for the benefit of present and future generations, through reasonable laws and other measures that

1. prevent pollution and ecological degradation (environmental disrepair);
2. promote conservation (preservation); and
3. secure ecologically sustainable development (growth that is wise and does not harm) and use of natural resources while promoting justifiable economic and social development. (In simple terms, the last sentence means human use of the environment should be good for the country's economy but should not harm the environment or humans in the short- or long-term.)

5

What is an activist?

Activists take action to bring about change. Environmental activists believe that the environment and all living things need to be protected. They learn and share their knowledge with others. They also take **direct action** to protect the environment.

Actions big and small
Some environmental activists focus on small actions, such as creating less trash. Others take on bigger projects, such as protecting forests, oceans, or wildlife. Activists accomplish their work by raising awareness and funds. They also put pressure on the people who have the power to change things, such as governments and businesses.

Looking at the big picture
Protecting Earth's environment is a huge job, but big changes can be made in small ways. For example, if a person **pledges** to travel by car 15 miles (24 kilometers) less each day, they could prevent almost half a ton (tonne) of pollution-creating **exhaust emissions** per year. Encouraging everyone to change their behavior is part of an environmental activist's work.

The pollution caused by car exhaust creates smog that makes it hard to breathe.

Who is an activist?
Some environmental activists are scientists who help educate people about pollution and waste. Other environmental activists raise funds for causes or stage protests. Anyone can be an environmental activist by doing research and caring about the environment.

Field Notes:

In 1997, environmental activist Julia Butterfly Hill was part of a campaign to save a forest in California. To protect the forest, she lived for two years in a redwood tree that loggers wanted to cut down. Hill brought media attention to her cause. The tree, called Luna, was saved from logging along with three acres (1.2 hectares) of forest around it. Here is what Julia wrote about her experience when she came down out of the tree.

"My first winter while living in Luna, I experienced the worst storms in the recorded history of California. At its most intense, winds were gusting 90 miles (145 kms) an hour. My tarp roof and walls had been completely torn apart. I was getting pummeled by rain and sleet, and getting thrown around by the wind. I was more frightened than I have ever been in my life. In this moment, I found the most profound (deep) state of grace when I embraced life to its fullest by embracing death. In that moment, I found a power and joy that is beyond words. My heart grieves deeply at the devastation we have wrought on our planetary family. I choose to address this with love and action."

—as told to E/The Environmental Magazine

How much is too much?

Everyone on Earth is a consumer. We consume natural resources, such as food and water. We also consume **fossil fuels**, such as oil, natural gas, and coal, to heat homes, cook food, and run cars. Using fossil fuels creates gases that harm the environment.

Examining consumption

Almost everything we make or buy comes from natural resources. In order to help the environment, activists must examine their own consumption habits, or how much and what they consume. Did you know that 20 percent of the world consumes 80 percent of the world's natural resources? Often, the people who consume the most are those who can afford to pay. But consuming more is not environmentally responsible because it creates waste.

What happens to our belongings when we are done with them? They become trash in a dump. The more belongings we have, the more trash we make.

Conserving and restoring

Environmentalists want to conserve natural resources, so that there is enough to go around. They also want to restore the environment that has been harmed by pollution. This means using less and saving more. Buying things made or grown locally means less pollution is created. Less energy is required to make and ship these goods. When consumer goods are packed for shipment and for sale, packaging materials made from paper and plastic are used. These materials must also be created and shipped. Some packaging is necessary to protect goods from being damaged. Other packaging is only meant to entice buyers. This excess packaging ends up as trash. More packaging equals more trash.

Get Active!

Celebrate World Buy Nothing Day

Buy Nothing Day is held near the end of November each year. There is one simple rule to observing this day, and that is to spend no money. The goal is to force people to think about what they consume. You can observe Buy Nothing Day by organizing an event at your school. One fun way to support it is to create a shopping-free zone— ask everyone to bring in things they do not want or use anymore to swap with others.

Living green

Living green means living in a sustainable way, or making as little impact on Earth as possible. Living in a sustainable way means maintaining the environment for the future. Cutting down trees faster than they can regrow is not a sustainable practice. But managing forests by planting new trees is a sustainable practice.

Rules for green living

Watering lawns to keep them green during a drought is not sustainable, but using rain barrels to capture rainwater for garden use is. Environmental activists also try to follow the important **principles** of sustainability: that everything we use or buy should be recycled, reused, remade, or buried in the ground where it can **decompose** and feed the soil.

Collecting rainwater in rain barrels is one way to cut down on water use and be more environmentally aware.

Get Active! Buyer Beware!

Many products sold in stores claim to be "green" or "eco-friendly." How can you make sure what you are buying is actually green? It is important to check product labels. Ask questions such as: What is the product made of? Does it save energy or water? Was pollution created in its manufacturing process? Can it be recycled? How far did it travel to get here? If you can't answer the questions easily, it might not be a green product after all.

10

Field Notes:

Bob Hunter was one of the co-founders of the environmental group Greenpeace. He began his career as a journalist. Throughout his life, he was involved in many environmental campaigns, including ones against whalers and seal hunters, nuclear weapons-makers, oil companies, and pesticide manufacturers. Bob Hunter believed that...

"...If we ignore [the] laws of ecology we will continue to be guilty of crimes against the Earth. We will not be judged by men for these crimes, but with a justice meeted out by the Earth itself. The destruction of the Earth will lead, inevitably, to the destruction of ourselves."

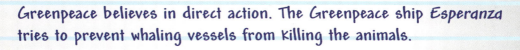

Greenpeace believes in direct action. The Greenpeace ship *Esperanza* tries to prevent whaling vessels from killing the animals.

A short history

In the past, humans did not worry too much about the environment. Ancient peoples did not have factories that created pollution. They also did not make plastics, drive cars, or use chemicals to fertilize their crops. Only in the last 300 years have humans begun to seriously harm the environment.

Industrialization

So what happened in the last 300 years? The world became more industrialized! The **Industrial Revolution** changed the way humans lived and how the environment was treated. By the mid-1800s, many North American cities were centers of industry. Factories burned coal for fuel. Burning coal pollutes the air with chemicals that harm the environment and human health.

Sierra Club founder John Muir was honored on a stamp. Parks, such as Yosemite (below), are a focus for the Sierra Club.

Early environmentalism

Industrialization changed the air and the land. Some people began to worry that if we continued to harm the environment, eventually the planet would not be able to support life. Early environmentalists were concerned with nature. In 1892, a group of **conservationists** headed by John Muir founded the Sierra Club, which became America's first and largest environmental organization. The club wanted to protect the country's wild places from destruction or **exploitation**. It **lobbied** the government to protect giant redwood trees in California, establish national parks, such as Yosemite National Park, and pass laws protecting the wilderness.

Changing the balance

The environment really began to change in the early 1900s, when oil was **refined** to produce everything from gasoline to paint and plastics. By the mid-1950s most families in North America owned their own vehicles. Cities began to sprawl out. Farmers began using modern fertilizers made from **petrochemicals** that produced more crops. Very few people thought about the consequences of growth and modernization. But this new way of life was damaging, the environment.

Silent Spring described how birds were being killed by pesticides.

The environmental movement

The modern environmental movement has its roots in the work of environmentalists, such as Rachel Carson in the 1950s. Carson worked for the U.S. Fish and Wildlife Service, and began to examine the effects of DDT, a chemical pesticide used to protect crops. Few people had given any thought about whether it was harmful. Carson wrote a book called *Silent Spring*. The book explained how DDT not only killed insects, but also killed birds and other animals in the food chain. *Silent Spring* is considered the spark that ignited a new generation of environmental activists.

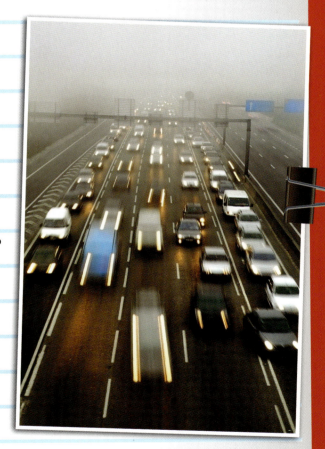

We are dependent upon pollution-creating automobiles.

Scientists warn that global warming could lead to the melting of the polar ice caps, rising sea levels, and changing weather patterns.

Environmental groups

Growing awareness about environmental issues and the desire to protect the planet's health led to the formation of many well-known environmental groups. Two of the biggest, Greenpeace and Friends of the Earth, were formed by groups of activists during the early 1970s. Both groups launched media campaigns that provided people with information about environmental issues, including pollution, the destruction of natural areas, and species at risk of **extinction**. These efforts led to an even greater awareness among the public and governments about how human activities were harming the planet.

Summits, conferences, and laws

In 1972, the United Nations Conference on the Human Environment was attended by representatives from 113 countries. They discussed topics such as industrial pollution, **acid rain**, and the health of the world's oceans. The summit showed that world leaders were starting to pay attention to Earth's environment and how it affected human health. The United Nations has organized an Earth Summit in every decade since 1972. At the Earth Summits, world leaders discuss pressing environmental issues and possible solutions.

Global warming

Throughout the 1980s, scientists and environmentalists were concerned about a growing hole in Earth's ozone layer. The ozone layer is a layer of the planet's **atmosphere** that protects living things from the Sun's harmful ultraviolet rays. This concern led to successful campaigns by environmental groups to ban the use of chemicals called CFCs, which destroy the ozone layer. CFCs were used in aerosol spray cans of products such as deodorants.

Today, many environmental activists are fighting global warming, which is an increase in Earth's temperature caused by the release of carbon dioxide into the atmosphere. Carbon dioxide is created by human use of fossil fuels, including the burning of coal to generate electricity and oil to power automobiles.

Get Active!

Form a grassroots group

Greenpeace began as a "grassroots" environmental movement. Grassroots groups start at the local level, not at the national level. All it takes is a few people concerned about a problem in their area to band together. Anyone can start a grassroots organization, including you. Find people in your area who have the same environmental concerns. Then try and recruit more people. Now you are on your way to starting your own grassroots organization.

Polar bears are threatened by melting Arctic ice caused by global warming.

On the land

Everything on Earth is connected in an **ecosystem**. Pollution on land affects the air, the water, and all living things. Our daily activities, such as throwing away trash and spraying chemical pesticides and fertilizers onto crops, jeopardizes the health of entire ecosystems. It has taken the efforts of many people, from ordinary citizens to ecologists and scientists, for us to realize this fact.

Leaking trash

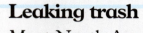

Most North Americans do not give their trash a second thought once it has left the curb. But what does happen to it, and why is it so bad? North Americans produce 70,000 trucks full of trash each day. The trash is picked up and driven many miles to a landfill site. At landfill sites, bulldozers move the trash so it is buried under the ground. It remains underground for hundreds of years, **leaching** chemicals into the soil and slowly rotting away. Some trash, such as Styrofoam, will never decompose. Activists have found many solutions to help control the trash problem. One that we are most familiar with today is the recycling program. Recycling cuts down on the waste sent to dumps and encourages people to think about what they are tossing away.

Spraying crops with chemical pesticides can have harmful effects in the long-term because pesticides threaten ecosystems.

Organic farming can be a form of environmental activism.

Soil food

One of the things activists most often find in trash is material that can be **composted**, such as leftover food, fruit and vegetable peelings, coffee grounds, and yard waste. When these things are returned to the soil, they give it nutrients—that is because they are "organic," or were once living. Many North American cities now have compost pick-up in addition to recycling and regular trash collection. People can also use compost on gardens as fertilizer. Some environmental activists argue that a method of farming called organic farming, which does not use chemical fertilizers or pesticides, is better for the environment.

Get Active!

Community gardens

Taking part in a community garden is a great way to learn more about how plants grow—and how humans depend on nature. A community garden is a garden, often on public land, that many people look after. Everyone shares in planting, watering, and weeding. When the gardens produce vegetables, they are shared by the gardeners. Ask your teacher or principal about planting a community garden at your school.

The air we breathe

If you go outside on a hot, smoggy summer day and take a deep breath, what happens? If the air around you seems to be covered in a brown haze, then you have just felt the effects of air pollution.

Acid rain can "kill" lakes. It can even damage buildings.

One way people can fight air pollution is to take public transportation.

Smog fighters

Around the world, cities are fighting the problem of smog, a mix of chemicals in the air that forms in part because of automobile exhaust and factory emissions. One of the most harmful forms of air pollution is the release of carbon dioxide into the atmosphere. Carbon dioxide is created when humans burn fossil fuels, such as oil and coal, to create energy. By driving a car, you are creating carbon dioxide. The release of too much carbon dioxide into the atmosphere is thought to be the main cause of global warming. Scientists believe carbon dioxide traps heat near Earth's surface, causing temperatures to rise.

Acid rain

Some pollution also causes acid rain. Acid rain is created when raindrops combine with sulfur and nitrogen from industrial emissions and become "acidified." When acid rain falls on an area, it can damage trees and other plants, harm animals, kill aquatic life, and make soil unsuitable for growing plants.

Field Notes:

On April 22, 1970, the first Earth Day was held in the United States. It was celebrated by over 20 million people. Almost 30 years later, Earth Day is being celebrated in 141 countries around the world. Senator Gaylord Nelson from Wisconsin started Earth Day as a form of grassroots activism. Here is what he had to say about the growth in environmentalism:

"You've got to consider how far we've come. In 1970 there wasn't any head of any corporation nurtured to think there was any such thing as an environmental problem. Nor was anybody else prepared to think that way. . . . Now you have heads of corporations who were raised after the environment became a popular concern. Many of them are very good environmentalists. I suppose one of the items that excites and irritates college students is greenwashing, people who aren't green trying to appear green." – Milwaukee Sentinel Journal, April 2001

Crowds celebrate Earth Day in a San Diego, California park.

19

Dirty water

Most of the water on Earth is found in the oceans. It is saltwater. Only about three percent of the water on the planet is freshwater, which is the water people drink. No living thing on Earth can survive without one of these types of water.

Say "no" to bottled water. It is better to help clean up your local water supply than to buy water in bottles. Bottles are plastics made from petrochemicals. They have to be manufactured and shipped. Plastic can be recycled, but this also uses energy. Often, plastic bottles are tossed in the trash, or worse, end up in streams and creeks (below).

Everybody needs it

Because water is essential to all life on Earth, environmentalists get a lot of support on the issue of water pollution. There are laws that protect water supplies but even with laws, environmentalists need to promote responsible water use. Preventing water pollution begins at home. A good place to start fighting water pollution is by never disposing of chemicals or other pollutants down a sink drain or toilet bowl. These substances can contaminate water supplies.

Get local

Organizing a campaign to raise awareness about water pollution in your school or neighborhood can also make a difference. To become a part of the larger fight against water pollution, research water quality in your town or city. A visit to your local library should be your first step. Ask a librarian to help you research. Write letters to government leaders asking them to ban pesticides and other harmful substances.

Think global

The Exxon Valdez oil spill is one of the world's best-known examples of water pollution. While traveling in Prince William Sound, Alaska, on March 24, 1989, the oil tanker Exxon Valdez struck a reef, spilling millions of gallons of oil into the Gulf of Alaska. The oil spill covered 11,000 square miles (23,490 square km), killing thousands of seabirds, fish, and other marine animals. The Exxon Valdez was an environmental disaster that focused attention on how easily the world's oceans can be polluted. Twenty years later, some scientists say the environment is still recovering.

Get Active!

Do not dump it down the drain

Check out the storm drains or sewers on your street. What goes down those drains and where does it go? Storm drains drain the street when it is raining or when snow melts so that the street does not flood. This water is called urban runoff. The water usually flows to the nearest creek or stream. Often, it is contaminated by dog feces, motor oil, grass clippings, or trash. Be a junior activist and encourage your parents and neighbors not to pollute the street and storm sewers.

Energy in need

Powering homes, businesses, and communities requires a massive amount of energy. Creating all of that energy has an effect on the environment including increasing global warming, air pollution, and wildlife habitat loss. Energy consumption is expected to increase in the future, and the world will face a challenge to meet its energy needs without destroying the environment. Global energy use is expected to rise by up to 50 percent by 2030.

Our brighter future?

Where does the world get all of the energy it needs to power industry and homes? About 80 percent of the world's energy is sourced from non-renewable fossil fuels. To make electricity, coal is burned, nuclear power is created, and the power of huge bodies of water is harnessed to create hydroelectricity. To heat our homes and businesses, we rely on oil and natural gas. The world's fossil fuel supply will not last forever. Environmentalists were among the first to point this out. One of the things environmentalists do is stress how we need to conserve energy now and seek out alternative forms of energy.

Smog created by burning fossil fuels makes it difficult for people to breathe.

Alternative energy

While the use of renewable "green" energy, such as solar and wind power, is growing, the majority of energy created by humans produces a negative impact on the environment. Ecosystems are changed forever when a dam is built to produce hydroelectricity, an oil development is created, a nuclear power plant is built, or a mine is dug for coal. Burning oil, gas, and coal to create energy creates smog and greenhouse gases. Nuclear waste, a **by-product** of using nuclear energy to generate electricity, can pose a grave danger to the environment.

Wind turbines use the power of wind to create electricity.

Get Active! Critical thinking

It is important to use critical thinking when discussing environmental issues. Critical thinking means thinking reasonably about something and evaluating before judging. Participate in a critical thinking exercise. Make a list of the things you do in a single day that require energy. Write ways you save energy and ways you use too much energy. What can you do to change? What do you think others can do to change their habits?

23

Environmental justice

Environmental justice is the fair treatment of all people regardless of their race, culture, or income when it comes to environmental laws and regulations. It is the idea that all people have the right to a clean environment, environmental protection, and a say in decisions that affect the environment where they live and work.

Toxic waste dumps are not usually located near expensive, gated neighborhoods.

The fight for rights

The concept of environmental justice is fairly new and grew from the desire of some environmentalists to make sure laws protected everyone regardless of race or economic status. They found that the poor, people of color, and **indigenous** groups suffered more often from poor water quality or chemical spills. Trash and toxic waste dumps were also located closer to their homes. They were more at risk for environmental hazards just because of who they were. This was an injustice that many called environmental racism. Many people throughout the world fight for environmental justice as a human right.

24

Field Notes:

Dr. Robert Bullard has been called the father of environmental justice. A university professor and activist who has written many books on environmental justice, Dr. Bullard is also the director of the Environmental Justice Resource Center at Clark Atlanta University. He believes that one of the tasks of an environmental justice advocate is to teach and empower people.

"The first line is that we have to start early. We have to educate young people that it is their right to have access to open space, parks, outdoors, as opposed to people thinking that they are supposed to be living in an area where the only park is a basketball court with no net. We have to give people this idea that it's their right to have access to open space and green space, and we have to provide funds to make sure that we get them early on and take them on field trips, take them to a wilderness area, a refuge, a reserve, to a park-a real park and to integrate this information into our curriculum."
– From an interview with Earth First! Journal

Seeing the beauty of nature can help foster an appreciation for it and the belief that parks are not just concrete playgrounds.

In the trenches

From grassroots environmentalists in your community, to royalty, the U.S. Vice-Presidency and Hollywood, environmental activists can be found everywhere. Here are just a few of the many:

Severn Cullis-Suzuki and David Suzuki

In 1992, a twelve-year-old Canadian girl addressed the delegates at the UN Earth Summit in Rio de Janeiro, Brazil. Her name was Severn Cullis-Suzuki, and she spoke out about the environment and the future. Three years earlier while on a family trip, Severn saw a portion of Brazil's Amazon forest being burned for farmland. The sight so affected her that when she returned to her school, she and five schoolmates formed an organization called the Environmental Children's Organization (ECO). Their purpose was to learn and teach other children about environmental issues.

Today, Severn still speaks out about the environment. She has also appeared as co-host on a television show with her father, environmental activist David Suzuki. A university professor for 40 years, and television host, David Suzuki has also written many books on science and nature. He has recieved many honors, including a United Nations Environment Program medal. The David Suzuki Foundation is an environmental organization he founded to examine climate change and sustainability.

Environmental activist David Suzuki often works with his daughter Severn Cullis-Suzuki.

26

Al Gore

Growing up in Washington, D.C. and Tennessee in the early 1960s, Al Gore remembers his mother reading Rachel Carson's *Silent Spring*. As a member of the U.S. House of Representatives, Gore brought the issues of climate change, toxic waste, and global warming to debates. He wrote articles for newspapers, held conferences, and ran on an election campaign based on clean air and water. In 2007, he was awarded a Nobel Peace Prize along with the Intergovernmental Panel on Climate Change for his efforts to fight climate change.

A former vice president of the United States, Al Gore is known for starring in the Academy-award winning documentary film *An Inconvenient Truth*.

Melissa Poe

When Melissa Poe was nine years old, she saw a TV show in which the characters were taken 25 years into the future. They witnessed a dead world, where there were no plants and everyone was dying because of pollution. This prompted Melissa to write to U.S. President George Bush asking him to help. When she was sent a form letter that did not even mention the environment in the response, Melissa took action. She convinced local businesses to post her letter on a billboard. In time, the letter spread, and her plea for the President's help to stop pollution appeared on 250 billboards across the country. Letters from other children began flooding in. Inspired by Melissa's letter, they wanted to know what they could do to help, too. Melissa formed Kids For A Clean Environment (Kids FACE) to encourage children to get involved in environmental action, from letter-writing to tree-planting.

What you can do

Composting is a good method of using kitchen waste to make fertilizer for plants.

Not every environmental activist is well-known. As any activist will tell you, the most important activism starts in the home. It is individuals, not businesses or governments, who will make the biggest impact of all when it comes to saving the planet. In environmental activism, actions speak as loud as words.

At home

There are some very simple ways you can help save the environment. You probably already recycle, but cutting down on the amount of waste you create is an even bigger step. You can make the effort to take your own reusable containers to the market to put food in, as well as use cloth bags instead of shopping bags. Always bring a backpack or other carry-all with your own drinking container and fork. Did you know that plastic forks and spoons and Styrofoam cups are **non-biodegradable**? See if you can go without having your trash collected for a month. How much trash is your household creating?

Ride your bike! Believe it or not, it is one of the easiest, quickest, and most fun ways to help the environment.

Many museums, nature centers, and national parks have environmental programs for kids where you can study nature or take water quality tests in streams.

In the community

There are many ways to take action for the environment in your own community. They can be simple things such as carpooling with teammates when you attend sports practices or games, or challenging your classmates to bring trashless lunches. A trashless lunch is a lunch that creates no trash through plastic bags or wrappers. Other community actions include organizing garage sales, recycling programs, and even field trips to recycling centers or landfill sites so people can see just how much waste is created and where it goes.

Get Active!

Get the word out!

Making your views known is an important step to making change happen. Global Response is an organization that uses letter-writing campaigns to address the environmental concerns of communities around the world. They make their members aware of an issue through newsletters and their Web site, and urge them to write letters to pressure businesses and governments to make good environmental decisions.
You can visit them on the Web at www.globalresponse.org to read about their latest campaigns.

Saving the planet

On this page, you will find Web sites of some well-known organizations that appear in this book. It is important that you view these sites with your teacher or parent. Some Web sites or links from these sites may contain topics and images of a sensitive nature. Discuss the information you read on these Web sites with your teacher or parent, and then make up your own mind about how you feel about the subject.

World Wildlife Fund (WWF)

With over five million members and conservation efforts in 100 countries, WWF is the world's largest conservation organization. Although it focuses mainly on saving animals and their habitats, WWF also works to help reduce pollution and overuse of Earth's resources. Find out how WWF works with local communities "In the Field" by visiting www.worldwildlife.org.

Greenpeace

It all began in an old fishing vessel headed from Vancouver, Canada, to an island off Alaska. The handful of environmentalists onboard were going to "bear witness" to nuclear testing in an attempt to save the birds and marine life in the area. From this event Greenpeace grew to become one of the world's most well-known independent global environmental organizations. Their daring protest tactics are intended to change attitudes and behaviors about the natural world and to influence others to protect and conserve the environment. Visit Greenpeace on the Web at www.greenpeace.org.

Worldwatch Institute

Worldwatch Institute is an independent research organization. Based in Washington, D.C., Worldwatch has researchers who study and write about issues of energy, climate change, sustainability, and ecology. The organization produces a magazine and other publications. Check their Web site out at www.worldwatch.org.

Sierra Club

America's oldest and largest environmental organization, the Sierra Club was formed in 1892. The Club's goal is conservation and protection of Earth's ecosystems. Visit their Web site at www.sierraclub.org.

Friends of the Earth

FOE is the world's largest grassroots environmental group. Visit their Web site to read the stories from countries around the world and to learn about environmental issues affecting the entire planet. You can also tune in to their Web-based radio station through the site. Check out www.foei.org.

GET ACTIVE!

31

Glossary

acid rain Rainfall that is environmentally harmful to lakes and rivers

atmosphere The gases that surround and protect Earth

by-product Something produced in addition to the main product

compost Vegetable matter that has been left to decay and turn into fertilizer for plants

conservationist A person who advocates or acts to protect the environment and wildlife

decompose To decay or rot

direct action Action taken by individuals or groups to make social change. Examples include strikes, protests, and sit-ins

ecosystem A group of living things and the environment they live in

entitled A claim someone has a right to

exhaust emissions The waste gases expelled from an automobile engine

exploitation To use and benefit unfairly from someone or something else

extinction When a species of animal or plant dies off

fossil fuels Fuels found in the earth, such as coal, oil, or gas

human rights The rights that belong to all humans

indigenous Something that is native or occurs naturally in an area

Industrial Revolution A period of rapid development in industry, building of factories and mass production of manufactured goods brought about by the invention of machines and steam power

leach To drain away in the soil

lobby To influence people and politicians

non-biodegradable Not able to be broken down by bacteria

petrochemicals Chemicals made from petroleum, or oil and gas

pledges A promise or undertaking

principles Rules that govern actions or behavior

refined A process where impurities are removed to make something

Index

acid rain 14, 18
air 4, 12, 16, 18, 22, 27
alternative energy 23
Bullard, Dr. Robert 25
Buy Nothing Day 9
Carson, Rachel 13, 27
conservation 5, 9, 12, 22, 30, 31
consumption 8, 9, 22
critical thinking 23
Cullis-Suzuki, Severn 26
Earth Day 19
environmental justice 24–25
environmental rights 4, 5, 24, 25
exhaust emissions 6, 18
Exxon Valdez 21
fossil fuels 8, 15, 18, 22, 23
Friends of the Earth 14, 31
Gore, Al 27
Greenpeace 11, 14, 15, 30
Hill, Julia Butterfly 7
human rights 5, 24
industrialization 12
Muir, John 12
organic farming 17
petrochemicals 13, 16, 17, 20
Poe, Melissa 27
Sierra Club 12, 31
Silent Spring 13, 27
sustainability 5, 10, 26, 31
Suzuki, David 26
trash 4, 6, 8, 9, 16, 17, 20, 21, 24, 28, 29
waste 6, 8, 16, 17, 23, 24, 27, 28, 29
water 4, 8, 10, 16, 17, 20, 24, 27, 29

Printed in China — CT